First published by Parragon in 2010
Parragon
Queen Street House
4 Queen Street
Bath BA1 1HE, UK

ISBN 978-1-4075-9043-1

Printed in China

Cinderella's Secret

Bath New York Singapore Hong Kong Cologne Delhi Melbourne

Are you good at keeping secrets? I hope you are, because I have a secret that no one knows - well, no one human, that is. I have a hiding place up in the castle attic.

Now that I'm married to the Prince, I am always busy going to fancy parties, planning banquets, and learning how to act like royalty. Who would have known that being a princess could be such hard work?

Luckily, I found a place I can escape to when I need a break from my Princess duties and want to be with my dearest little friends. The best part is that it's my very own secret hiding spot!

I have lots of parties in my secret room.
The mice and I share tea while they tell me
all the news from the village. Once, Suzy told
me that the butcher had fallen in love with the
tavern keeper's daughter. They were planning a
beautiful garden wedding!

Gus loves to hear about the royal banquets I attend. I tell him stories about dining with kings and queens and how we use a different fork for every course - sometimes I eat with eight forks during one meal! Of course, talking about food always makes Gus hungry.

I keep my trunk of treasures in my secret hiding place. It's filled with my favourite books, beautiful fabrics, and keepsakes from my mother. Even the glass slipper that led me to marry the Prince is safely tucked away in my trunk.

I keep a scrapbook in my secret place too!
I fill it with pressed flowers from the castle grounds, love
letters from the Prince, and funny pictures that Suzy likes
to draw of me and our friends.

Sometimes we eat cookies that I make from my mother's old recipe book. We share them with the birds on the window ledge. They wouldn't let out a peep about my secret place!

Once, when I wasn't there, Pom-Pom, the castle's cat, found her way to my hidden staircase and almost made it to the attic. Luckily, the mice heard her. They sent one of the birds to get my dog, Bruno, quickly!

Bruno charged up the stairs and chased
Pom-Pom back down. That was a close one!
I would hate it if anyone found my secret hiding spot!

The mice love to play dress-up, and my hiding spot is the perfect place for it. I make them little costumes to laugh and play in. When I tell them funny stories about castle life, they put on their tiny outfits and pretend they are kings and queens. They are so cute!

I love to sew, especially in the castle attic. Sometimes I open my mother's book of patterns and close my eyes, and whatever my finger lands on is the item I make. One day, my finger landed on a beautiful scarf. I knew just who to make it for: my loving Prince!

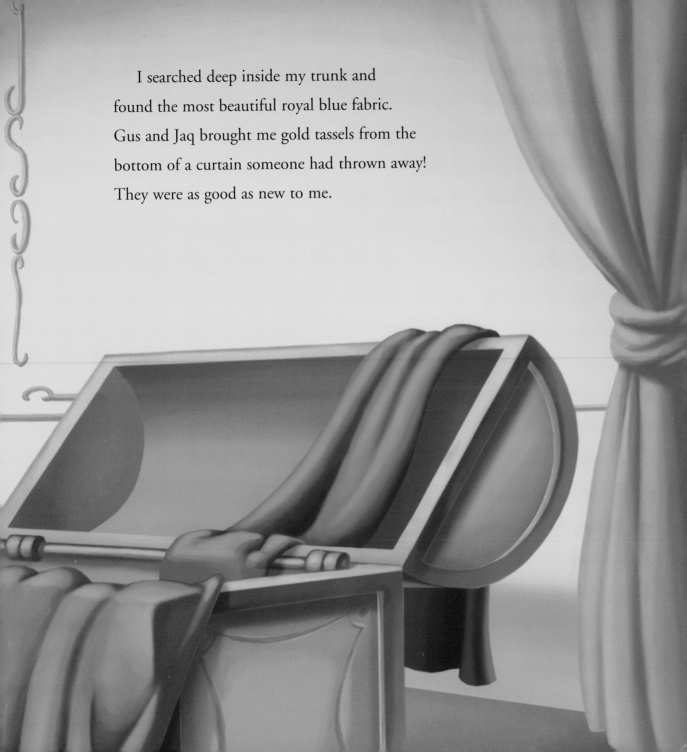

I searched deep inside my trunk and
found the most beautiful royal blue fabric.
Gus and Jaq brought me gold tassels from the
bottom of a curtain someone had thrown away!
They were as good as new to me.

The mice and I worked very hard on this special gift. Suzy
helped me sew. Gus and Jaq smoothed the wrinkles out with
their tiny hands.

Finally, the scarf was done. We all agreed it was the handsomest scarf we had ever seen - almost as handsome as my Prince!

When I gave the Prince his gift, he smiled and kissed me.

He wore his new scarf as proudly as he wears his crown.

It looked perfect on him! Suzy, Gus, and Jaq clapped with glee.

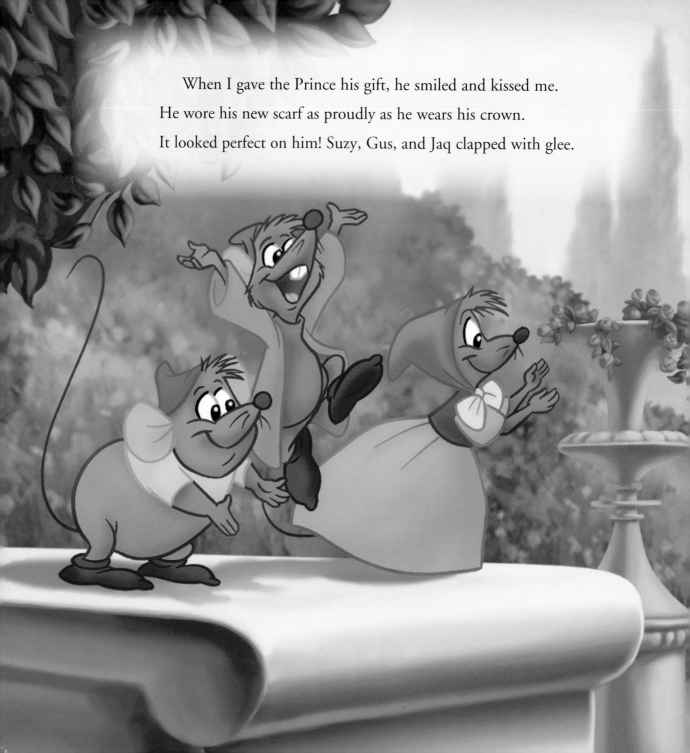

I am very good at keeping my attic room a secret.
My love for the Prince is much harder to hide!